D0432144

For Emily and Henry

Thanks to Kelvinside Kindergarten for their artistic hamster drawings
and to Colours Model Agency for the children.

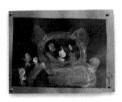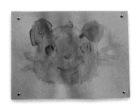

Henry Holt and Company, LLC
Publishers since 1866
175 Fifth Avenue
New York, New York 10010
mackids.com

Library of Congress Cataloging-in-Publication Data
Freytag, Lorna, author, illustrator.
My humongous hamster goes to school / Lorna Freytag. — First American edition.
pages   cm
"First published in the United Kingdom in 2014 by Piccadilly Press"—Copyright page.
Summary: On Bring Your Pet to School Day, a boy's hamster grows to enormous size
after he eats all the packed lunches.
ISBN 978-1-62779-140-3 (hardback)
[1. Hamsters—Fiction. 2. Size—Fiction. 3. Pets—Fiction. 4. Schools—Fiction.] I. Title.
PZ7.F894MyK 2015   [E]—dc23   2014029345

Henry Holt books may be purchased for business or promotional use. For information
on bulk purchases, please contact the Macmillan Corporate and Premium Sales Department
at (800) 221-7945 x5442 or by e-mail at specialmarkets@macmillan.com.

First published in the United Kingdom in 2014 by Piccadilly Press
First American edition—2015
Printed in China by WKT Company Limited, New Territories, Hong Kong

1   3   5   7   9   10   8   6   4   2

MY HUMONGOUS HAMSTER

HAMSTER

WITHDRAWN

GOES TO SCHOOL

Lorna Freytag

Henry Holt and Company • New York

Today is
"bring your pet
to school" day.

So I bring my hamster.

Freddy brings his fish.
Maisie brings her rabbit.

My hamster has never
been to school before.

My hamster gets out of his cage—
he must be hungry!

He eats my packed lunch.
He eats **EVERYONE'S**
packed lunch.

And then my hamster
begins to **GROW**
and
GROW...

...until he is

HUMONGOUS!

The teacher tells my hamster
to sit down and behave.

When the bell rings,
it's time for music
and dance class.

My hamster
wants to dance, too.
He likes it when we twirl.

In art class, I draw my hamster.
EVERYONE draws my hamster.

When we ask him which one he likes best, he **EATS** all the drawings!

He wanders down the hall
and peers into each classroom.

He surprises the lunch ladies in the cafeteria

and eats **ALL** the lunches.

Then he climbs on
the gym equipment.

After a while, my hamster goes outside to play hopscotch.

He takes a turn on the slide...

...and spins on the
merry-go-round!

After such a busy day,
my hamster is very tired

and wants to go home.

The whole class gives him a hug
to make him feel better.

Bit by bit,

my hamster shrinks back

to normal hamster size.

Now he can go home.

When Mom picks us up,
she asks if I've had a nice day.

I just say, "Nah, it was boring."

I don't want to get my
hamster in trouble, do I?